ENCOUNTER

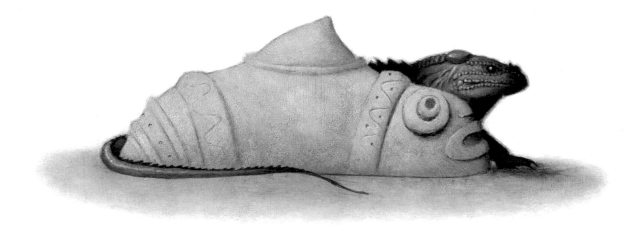

WRITTEN BY

JANE YOLEN

ILLUSTRATED BY

DAVID SHANNON

VOYAGER BOOKS
HARCOURT BRACE & COMPANY
SAN DIEGO   NEW YORK   LONDON

Requests for permission to make copies of any part of the work
should be mailed to: Permissions Department,
Harcourt Brace & Company, 6277 Sea Harbor Drive,
Orlando, Florida 32887-6777.

First Voyager Books edition 1996
Voyager Books is a registered trademark of Harcourt Brace & Company.

Library of Congress Cataloging-in-Publication Data
Yolen, Jane.
Encounter/written by Jane Yolen; illustrated by David Shannon.
p.   cm.
"Voyager Books."
Summary: A Taino Indian boy on the island of San Salvador recounts
the landing of Columbus and his men in 1492.
ISBN 0-15-225962-7
ISBN 0-15-201389-X pb
1. Taino Indians—Juvenile fiction.   [1. Taino Indians—Fiction.
2. Indians of the West Indies—Fiction.   3. Columbus, Christopher—
Fiction.]   I. Shannon, David, 1959–   ill.   II. Title.
PZ7.Y58En   1992
[Fic]—dc20   91-23746

B D F G E C

Printed in Singapore

The paintings in this book were done in acrylic.
The text type was set in Cloister by Thompson Type, San Diego, California.
Color separations by Bright Arts, Ltd., Singapore
Printed and bound by Tien Wah Press, Singapore
Production supervision by Warren Wallerstein and Pascha Gerlinger
Designed by Lisa Peters

For Marilyn
for twenty-seven years
—J. Y.

To my wife, Heidi,
and in memory of John Nissen
—D. S.

The moon was well overhead, and our great fire had burned low. A loud clap of thunder woke me from my dream.

All dreams are not true dreams, my mother says. But in my dream that night, three great-winged birds with voices like thunder rode wild waves in our bay. They were not like any birds I had ever seen, for sharp, white teeth filled their mouths.

I left my hammock and walked to the beach. There were my dream birds again. Only now they were real — three great-sailed canoes floating in the bay. I stared at them all through the night.

When the sun rose, each great canoe gave birth to many little ones that swam awkwardly to our shore.

I ran then and found our chief still sleeping in his hammock.

"Do not welcome them," I begged him. "My dream is a warning."

But it is our custom to welcome strangers, to give them the tobacco leaf, to feast them with the pepper pot, and to trade gifts.

"You are but a child," our chief said to me. "All children have bad dreams."

The baby canoes spat out many strange creatures, men but not men. We did not know them as human beings, for they hid their bodies in colors, like parrots. Their feet were hidden, also.

And many of them had hair growing like bushes on their chins.

Three of them knelt before their chief and pushed sticks into the sand.

Then I was even more afraid.

Our young men left the shelter of the trees. I — who was not yet a man — followed, crying, "Do not welcome them. Do not call them friends."

No one listened to me, for I was but a child.

Our chief said, "We must see if they are true men." So I took one by the hand and pinched it. The hand felt like flesh and blood, but the skin was moon to my sun.

The stranger made a funny noise with his mouth, not like talking but like the barking of a yellow dog.

Our chief said to us, "See how pale they are. No one can be that color who comes from the earth. Surely they come from the sky."

Then he leaped before them and put his hands up, pointing to the sky, to show he understood how far they had flown.

"Perhaps they have tails," said my older brother. "Perhaps they have no feet."

Our young men smiled, but behind their hands so the guests would not feel bad. Then they turned around to show that *they* had no tails.

Our chief gave the strangers balls of cotton thread to bind them to us in friendship. He gave them spears that they might fish and not starve. He gave them gum-rubber balls for sport. He gave them parrots, too — which made our young men laugh behind their hands all over again, knowing it was our chief's little joke, that the strangers looked like parrots.

But the strangers behaved almost like human beings, for they laughed, too, and gave in return tiny smooth balls, the color of sand and sea and sun, strung upon a thread. And they gave hollow shells with tongues that sang *chunga-chunga*. And they gave woven things that fit upon a man's head and could cover a boy's ears.

For a while I forgot my dream.

For a while I was not afraid.

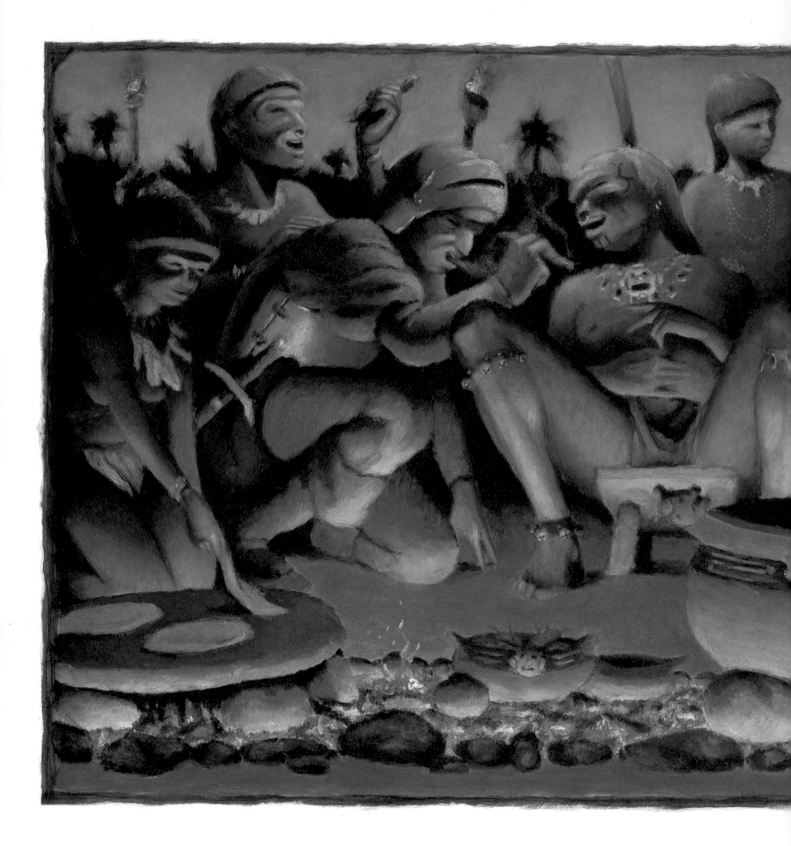

So we built a great feasting fire and readied the pepper pot and
yams and cassava bread and fresh fish. For though the strangers were
not quite human beings, we would still treat them as such.

Our chief rolled tobacco leaves and showed them how to smoke, but they coughed and snorted and clearly did not know about these simple things.

Then I leaned forward and stared into their chief's eyes. They were blue and gray like the shifting sea.

Suddenly, I remembered my dream and stared at each of the strangers in turn. Even those with dark human eyes looked away, like dogs before they are driven from the fire.

So I drew back from the feast, which is not what one should do, and I watched how the sky strangers touched our golden nose rings and our golden armbands but not the flesh of our faces or arms. I watched their chief smile. It was the serpent's smile — no lips and all teeth.

I jumped up, crying, "Do not welcome them."

But the welcome had already been given.

I ran back under the trees, back to the place where my *zemis* stood. I fed it little pieces of cassava, and fish and yam from the feast. Then I prayed.

"Let the pale strangers from the sky go away from us."

My *zemis* stared back at me with unblinking wood eyes. I gave it the smooth balls a stranger had dropped in my hand.

"Take these eyes and see into the hearts of the strangers from the sky. If it must be, let something happen to me to show our people what they should know."

My *zemis* was silent. It spoke only in dreams. Indeed, it had spoken to me already.

When I returned to the feast, one of the strangers let me touch his sharp silver stick. To show I was not afraid, I grasped it firmly, as one would a spear. It bit my palm so hard the blood cried out. But still no one understood; no one heard.

They did not hear because they did not want to listen. They desired all that the strangers had brought: the sharp silver spear; round pools to hold in the hand that gave a man back his face; darts that sprang from sticks with a sound like thunder that could kill a parrot many paces away.

We were given none of these — only singing shells and tiny balls on strings. We were patted upon the head as a child pats a yellow dog. We were smiled at with many white teeth, a serpent's smile.

The next day the strangers returned to their great canoes. They took five of our young men and many parrots with them. They took me.

I knew then it was a sign from my *zemis,* a sign for my people. So I was brave and did not cry out. But I *was* afraid.

That night, while my people slept on shore, the great-sailed canoes left our bay, going farther and farther than even our strongest men could go. Soon the beach and trees and everything I knew slipped away, until my world was only a thin, dark line stretched between sky and sea.

What else was there to do?

In the early morning, another land lay close enough to see. Silently, I let myself over the side of the great canoe. I fell down and down and down into the cold water. Then I swam to that strange shore.

Many days I walked, following the sun. Many nights I swam. And many times the sky was full with the moon and stars.

All along the way I told the people of how I had sailed in the great canoes. I told of the pale strangers from the sky. I said our blood would cry out in the sand. I spoke of my dream of the white teeth.

But even those who saw the great canoes did not listen, for I was a child.

So it was we lost our lands to the strangers from the sky. We gave our souls to their gods. We took their speech into our mouths, forgetting our own. Our sons and daughters became *their* sons and daughters, no longer true humans, no longer ours.

That is why I, an old man now, dream no more dreams. That is why I sit here wrapped in a stranger's cloak, counting the stranger's bells on a string, telling my story. May it be a warning to all the children and all the people in every land.

Author's Note

When Christopher Columbus landed on San Salvador, his first landfall in the New World, on October 12, 1492, he claimed the beautiful little green island for his king and queen and country. Yet it was not an uninhabited island upon which he set the Spanish flag. The Taino lived there and called the place *Guanahani* after the island's many iguanas. The Taino were a gentle people who wore gold nose rings and gold armbands, sometimes painted their faces and bodies, and always greeted strangers with a feast.

Columbus called the tribespeople "Indians," mistaking the land for India. In his journal, he wrote that they were "well made, with fine shapes and faces; their hair short, and coarse like that of a horse's tail, combed toward the forehead, except a small portion which they suffer to hang down behind. . . . "

The Taino gave the sailors balls of cotton thread and fish darts and parrots in friendship. In turn, the sailors gave them Venetian glass beads, little brass bells, and red caps. They asked in sign where the natives' gold rings and armbands came from. It was the gold that interested them the most.

Columbus carried away ten young Taino men and women (or six, according to different sources) from the various islands they visited, carting them back to Spain as slaves. Later when the islands were colonized by the Spanish, the native religions, languages, and lifestyles were changed forever. Though there were originally some 300,000 native islanders, by 1548 — a little more than fifty years later — less than 500 remained. Today, there are no full-blooded Taino.

Since most stories about that first encounter are from Columbus's point of view, I thought it would interest readers to hear a Taino boy speak. We don't have an actual record of that, so I have re-created what he might have said — using historical records and the storyteller's imagination.

Illustrator's Note

Creating illustrations for this book presented many challenges, because little is known about the Taino culture. Apparently most of their artifacts were either melted down or burned; those that are left are made of stone. Many mysteries remain — such as the meaning of the fin-shaped stone *zemis* on page 1. As far as we know, the native people wore no clothing, so I was faced with the problem of how to present them without offending those who object to nudity in a children's book. I chose to portray them with a cloth covering to be as accurate as possible without interfering with the story.